YP SM
Smith, Alex T.
Foxy and Egg : a book / by A
M   380689

WITHDRAWN
SEP 19 2024

P9-ANZ-291

The author wishes to thank
MISS KATHRYN MILTON and MISS HOLLY SMITH,
and ALISON ELDRED for all her egg-cellent help.

Holiday House *presents* FOXY AND EGG
Starring VIVIEN VIXEN *and* EDWARD L'OEUF
Costarring MARLON BITEHARD
Directed by ALEX T. SMITH

Chicken showgirls appear courtesy of *The Rosecomb Sisters*
"Shake Your Tail Feathers" Dance Troupe.

Text and illustrations copyright © by Alex T. Smith 2010
First released in 2010 by Hodder Children's Books, 338 Euston Road, London NW1 3BH
The right of Alex T. Smith to be identified as the author and the illustrator of this Work has been
asserted by him in accordance with the Copyright, Designs and Patents Act 1988.
First published in the United States of America by Holiday House in 2011
All Rights Reserved
HOLIDAY HOUSE is registered in the U.S. Patent and Trademark Office.
Printed and bound in November 2011 in Dongguan, Guangdong, China, at SCPC Ltd.
www.holidayhouse.com
First American Edition
1 3 5 7 9 10 8 6 4 2

Library of Congress Cataloging-in-Publication Data
Smith, Alex T.
Foxy and Egg / by Alex T. Smith. — 1st American ed.
p. cm.
Summary: Foxy DuBois is delighted when Egg rolls up to her door, and she invites him in
to enjoy dinner, games, and a place to sleep, even as she makes plans for a special breakfast.
ISBN 978-0-8234-2330-9 (hardcover)
[1. Foxes—Fiction. 2. Eggs—Fiction. 3. Hospitality—Fiction. 4. Humorous stories.]
I. Title.
PZ7.S6422Fox 2011
[E]—dc22
2010026416

A COPRODUCTION BETWEEN HOLIDAY HOUSE AND FOX AND HOUND PICTURES.

A book by
ALEX T. SMITH

FOXY AND EGG

Starring

VIVIEN VIXEN
as FOXY DuBOIS

Introducing

EDWARD L'OEUF
as EGG

HOLIDAY HOUSE / NEW YORK

Of all the suspicious-looking
houses in all the deserted woods in
all the world, he had to roll up to hers. . . .

Foxy DuBois was utterly charming
and always kind to strangers, so she
invited Egg in for a BITE to eat.

While Foxy skipped off to the kitchen,
Egg rocked and rolled around the grand house.
"You have some interesting paintings," shouted Egg.
But Foxy wasn't listening.
She was too busy cooking up a perfectly cunning plan. . . .

Foxy wanted
the biggest, most
delicious egg to eat,
so she put part one
of her conniving plan
into action: she
would fatten Egg up!

When dinner was
served, it was a
very splendid affair.
Egg wobbled
with excitement.

Foxy wanted a big egg,
but she also wanted a
fit egg, so, after dinner,
she put part two
of her devious plan
into action: they
played games.

They had
an egg-and-
spoon race
in the hallway

and played hide-
and-seek in
the library

followed by
musical chairs in
the drawing room.

At the end of the night,
Egg was in a complete spin!
It had been a delightful
evening, but he needed to
rest his weary shell.

"You simply must stay over,"
said Foxy.
"I have something
even more wonderful
planned for breakfast!"

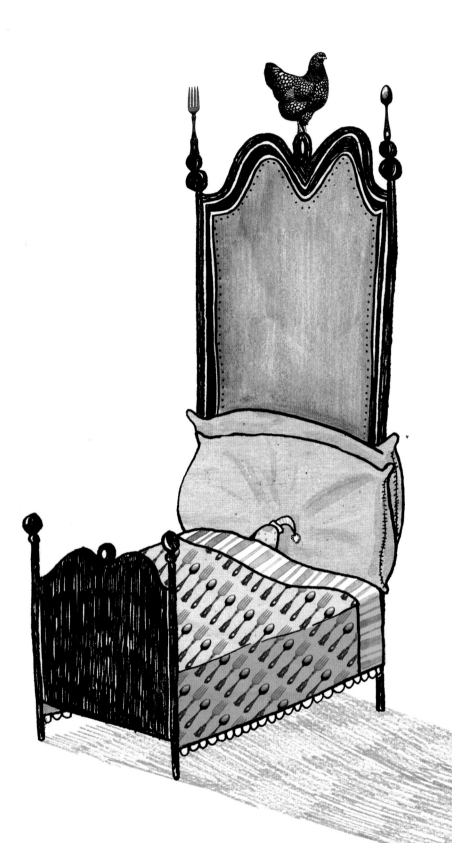

As Egg snuggled
down in his cozy bed,
Foxy spent the night
dreaming eggy dreams. . . .

There were
scrambled eggs
and fried eggs,
poached eggs
and baked eggs,
and, best of all,
soft-boiled eggs
and toast!

But when
Foxy DuBois
awoke the next
morning, she was
in for a shock. . . .

During the night something had changed.
Egg was a fragile little thing no more. He was

ENORMOUS!

Foxy rubbed her hands with glee;
her crafty plan had worked.
It was going to be a big breakfast. . . .

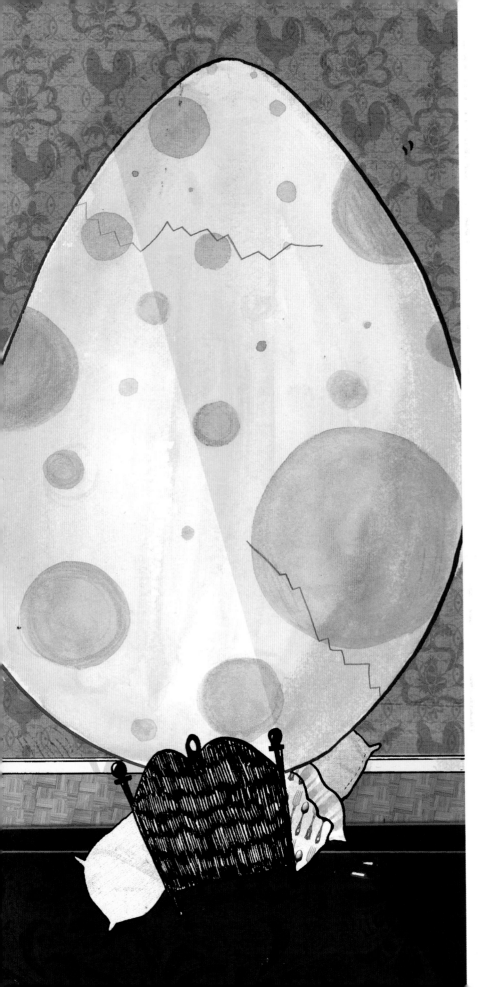

But just then Egg started to

CRACK!

Foxy licked her lips.

CRACK!

She licked her lips some more.
Then with one final crack,
Foxy saw what was inside. . . .

"Good morning!"
said Alphonso wickedly.

"Am I in time for
breakfast?"

The End